RECKLESS WOLF'S DANGEROUS LIAISON

COMPANY 417 SHIFTERS SERIES

AMELIA WILSON

CONTENTS

Chapter 1   1
Chapter 2   7
Chapter 3   13
Chapter 4   18
Chapter 5   24
Chapter 6   30
Chapter 7   36
Chapter 8   41
Chapter 9   48
Chapter 10   53
Chapter 11   59
Epilogue   65

CHAPTER ONE

Carmella

It's another day.

It's always another day.

I remember my mom's saying. The sun will still rise tomorrow. She said that all the time and she meant it as an encouragement, as a way to remember that no matter how bad things get, life goes on. I guess there's some encouragement in that but, frankly, I'm not feeling it lately.

The strangest thing about it all is that life isn't getting bad for me. Not at all. I guess, I'm pretty successful, actually. I'm co-owner of a successful import company that gives me a very comfortable life. My two partners are my best friends, and all of the warnings about business ruining friendships never came true. On the contrary, I still love Diane and Kim and love them just like I have our whole lives since we ended up friends back in elementary school.

I guess most people would be happy to have my life.

But it's just one day happening after another and I don't know what I'm missing. All I know is I wake up not feeling particularly happy and not feeling particularly sad. I don't have any drama in my life and I don't have any joy in my life. I just exist.

And it's another day.

The fact that this particular day is a day at a resort on a beautiful lake doesn't make it any better for me. I don't know what my problem is. Diane and Kim are living it up, laughing and pointing out everything and everyone. Sure, I play along, but I don't share any of their excitement.

And damn it all to Hell, I don't know why!

There's no reason at all for me to not be excited. It isn't like today is boring or rotten or anything at all like that. I just can't shake this feeling of... what's that word for it? I think it's *ennui*. I mean, I'm pretty sure *ennui* is like a life where everything just seems boring and worthless or something. I don't know and I'm not really motivated to look it up.

I'm not really motivated to do anything, for Christ's sake.

I don't understand why, either. It's not like I don't have a lot of reasons to be happy with my life. I don't know why everything just seems boring and... Well, boring isn't even the right way to put it. It's just...

Well, I once watched a few minutes of a documentary

about drug addiction. Evidently there's something that can happen to long term drug abusers called *anti-hedonism* or *ahedonism* or *non-hedonism* or something like that. The point is nothing gives them pleasure. Nothing excites them. They've reached a point where there just isn't any joy at all.

I've never done drugs recreationally and I've never done drugs of any significance for medical reasons. Nonetheless, that not hedonistic thing I watched on the show caught my interest because that's exactly how I feel. It's like nothing in life really brings me any happiness or gets me excited at all.

Diane shrieks with delight and I turn to see her and Kim taking turns diving into the lake. When Diane comes up from her dive, she calls to me. "Carmella, swim with us!"

I put on a fake smile and lift my drink. "Can't, I'm too sober!"

"Drink by the lake!" Kim says.

I instead sip my tasteless drink at the bar and make exaggerated motions and noises of enjoyment as my friends continue to beg.

"Come on, Carmie!"

"Please!"

"We're so bored without you!"

When this doesn't succeed in swaying me, they charm a few poor, innocent boys and rope them into chanting, "Carmie! Carmie!"

I'm impressed enough at their dedication that I actually decide to join them. Why not let them enjoy themselves, at least?

I turn around to announce my surrender when I see a trail of smoke on the far side of the lake. I stand and stare into the distance. The smoke is coming from a large luxury houseboat near the far shore of the lake.

I'm not sure at first what is happening. At first, I think that maybe someone is barbecuing but there seems to be too much smoke for that. My second thought is that someone is having a bonfire or cookout on the opposite shore and the boat is just blocking the view. I think my mind just doesn't want to accept what I'm really seeing.

Then I see the flames and I can't pretend anymore.

"Fire!" I shout. I run toward the lake, shrieking, "Fire! Fire!"

Everyone stops cheering and stares uncertainly. Kim and Diane roll their eyes. They think I'm pranking them.

"That boat's on fire!" I scream.

Kim's and Diane's smiles fade. They turn and as soon as they see the flames, they scream and run out of the lake. The rest of the crowd discovers the fire and flees as well. I reach the end of the lake and realize that no one has called for help.

Then I realize I left my cell phone at the bar.

"Dammit!" I shout.

I run back toward the bar, shouting "Call 911!"

The bartender looks toward me and sees the fire. His eyes widen. He cries out, "Oh, shit!" and fumbles for his phone.

Why hadn't I thought of that in the first place?

I'm halfway back to the bar when I hear someone shout, "Look!"

I turn and see a small boat racing toward the houseboat. I can hear the roar of the fire and my stomach turns.

Then I see a god jump out of the motorboat.

He dives into the water and swims to the houseboat and the sun seems to literally sparkle off of his back. His body is chiseled and bronzed and his features seem cut from marble. He reaches the boat and climbs up a ladder on the side, then rushes into the burning boat.

The people gathered on shore exclaim and I feel my stomach turn again. I'm not sure why I should fear so much for the safety of this man whom I have never met but I feel profound relief when I see him emerge with a middle-aged man who I assume is the owner of the boat. The two of them quickly lower the lifeboat into the water. The older man climbs down the ladder into the boat and starts the engine while the god runs back to the cabin and returns with a middle-aged woman. A young couple follows behind. The mother is carrying a baby. The god holds another one.

By the time the fireboats arrive, everyone is safely in the lifeboat. The god motions for the lifeboat to drive away, then dives into the water. A few seconds later, there's a loud cracking noise and the houseboat lists heavily to one side.

I stare at the water, my heart pounding. Where is he?

Finally, I see him resurface a few dozen yards from

the boat. One of the fireboats picks him up while the other extinguishes the flame. I see the captain of the fireboat shake the god's hand and speak briefly to him. They're too far away to hear, but it's clear the captain is thanking the god and telling him that if he hadn't been there, everyone on that houseboat would have died.

"Wow," Diane breathed.

"He's hot," Kim added.

I can't say the feeling in my chest is entirely lust, but lust is definitely a part of it. It feels good, whatever it is. After feeling nothing for so long, feeling anything at all is wonderful.

"Yes," I agree. "He is."

CHAPTER TWO

Fort

"Damn it all to hell, Gilmore!" Tommy shouts. "There's no way out!"

"I want hoses on the windows and two volunteers to follow me," I reply as I step forward.

For all Tommy's irritation, I hear him say immediately, "Behind you." Another voice says the same. I think it's Brett but I'm not sure. The smoke is thick and the axe feels good in my hands. I get through the hallway, wincing at the heat I can feel even through my protective gear.

"Thank God," the voice I'm not confident belongs to Brett says. The door we're after is cracked open. That means there's no chance of a backdraft or a blast. I can see fire along the walls and I can almost sense the civilians in the room. I move forward and kick the door the rest of the way open. Six or seven frightened kids are against the wall.

Jesus, I'm turning into my parents. Every one of these people in in their early twenties and I'm thinking of them as kids.

"Get them to the corner!" I shout. I sense rather than see Brett and Tommy do as I say. I head to the window and see water running down over it. "Breaking a window," I say. "Get the basket over here." The building is old, so my axe makes short work of the window but I have to break away jagged glass along the edges in order to make it safe. "Where's my basket?"

"Flag us." I hold the axe out the window and wave it a bit. "We got you," comes the voice. By then, we've got the kids somewhat organized. I check around and satisfy myself the place isn't going to collapse. A moment later, I see the basket against the window. I nod to Brett who takes the arm of one of the girls and uses his other arm for the next.

He walks them over as I say, "Tommy, one more."

One of the college guys steps forward. Tommy moves him to the side and takes the last of the girls. It's not protocol officially that women come out first but it's still the way we do things. Children and women first. Maybe it's old fashioned but we're old-fashioned guys. I get them into the basket. Lopez is inside and he steadies them as the basket goes down. When the basket comes back up, I figure we can get all four of the remaining guys in.

"Can we make it out or should we wait for the

basket?" I ask as it heads back to the ground. As though the building decides to respond for us, there's a deafening boom and the whole place shakes like crazy. "What happened?" I shout.

The radio squawks and then I hear sergeant Holstein's voice (and the way we make fun of him for having a name like Holstein as a wolf shifter, you can't even imagine) saying, "That was a propane tank on the porch. We don't know what structural damage it caused."

I see the crew on the ground trying to hurry the other survivors out of the basket. The building groans and I know the basket won't make it up in time.

"Forget the basket!" I call into my radio. To Tommy and Brett, I say, "You each take two guys and follow me. We have to evacuate through the building."

"Gilmore!" my radio squeals. "You stay where you are and wait for the basket! Don't you dare go into that building!"

"No time, Captain," I reply. I motion for Tommy and Brett to follow and leave the room.

Smoke lies thick and I motion for everyone to stay low. We crouch and I lead everyone to where the smoke seems thinnest. I have to move slowly so the four evacuees can keep up and I feel my heart pounding as the building groans again.

We reach a stairwell and I check the door for heat. I feel coolness and usher everyone inside. We travel down six flights to the ground floor and I check for heat. The door is baking hot.

"Dammit," I mutter. "Upstairs!" I call to everyone, then lead them to the second floor.

The door is cool and I run to a window. It opens to a hedge that isn't burning yet. Better a few scratches then burning to death. I explain to Tommy and Brett. Brett shakes his head but agrees to jump first to help catch the evacuees.

The building groans again and shifts, so slightly as to be barely perceptible but perceptible nonetheless. Tommy and I exchange a look, then quickly help the evacuees exit. Once they hit the ground, Brett directs them to run toward the waiting paramedics on the road.

After the last evacuee leaves, Tommy rolls through the window and through to a dead run toward the engines.

The building groans and shifts again and I jump. Like Tommy, I roll straight through to a dead run and Brett and I sprint toward the engines. Halfway to the road, the building groans again, much louder and deeper than before.

A second later, we hear the first crashing booms of debris as the building collapses inward. We reach the road and nearly collide with the waiting paramedics. As they check us for injuries, Captain Yates marches over, scowling.

"Gilmore!" he calls. "What the hell do you think you were doing?"

"Saving lives, sir," I respond.

He continues to scowl but there's a hint of a smile as

well when he barks, "Once the medics fix you up, I want you in my office, ASAP!"

"Yes, sir," I say, offering a faint smile of my own.

Yates is still scowling when I step into his office thirty minutes later. He looks up at me and frowns. "One of these days, you're going to get yourself killed."

"The basket wouldn't have made it in time," I say. "We only had one way out."

Yates sighs. "There's a reason we have protocols, Gilmore. We do things the way we do them because it works."

"Yes, sir," I say. "Until it doesn't."

He stares at me a moment, then chuckles. He shakes his head and says, "I have to pretend to discipline you or the chief will have my ass." He tosses two twenties onto the desk. "You're taking the night off. Drinks are on me."

I smile. "Thank you, Yates. I'll see you tomorrow."

"Evening," Yates says.

"Tomorrow evening," I confirm.

"Just making sure we're on the same page."

I leave the office to a chorus of cheers from the other firefighters. Tommy and Brett embrace me on my way out and we promise to go hunting together when we can have some off-duty time.

I head to a lakeside bar on the north shore, a favorite little spot of mine a few hundred yards from the marina. The bartender there makes the best long island iced tea I've ever had but it's not the drinks on my mind as I walk toward the bar.

The girl sitting at the bar is the most beautiful creature I've ever seen. If a fairy tale princess married an angel, their daughter could not be more beautiful than this woman. She has a body men dream about, long, flowing hair and elegant features that seem almost impossible to believe.

I walk to the bar as if in a trance and stand next to her. "Hey," I say.

She turns to me and her eyes widen slightly, almost as if she recognizes me although we've never met. "Hey," she replies.

I smile at her. "Buy you a drink?"

CHAPTER THREE

Carmella

"You know," I say, "I saw you in action."

"In action?"

"Sure. You're a hero." I can tell he has no idea what I mean, and as I look at his eyes, I realize the humility he displays is sexy as fuck. I haven't been attracted to anyone in a long time. Oh, sure, I notice people are attractive but that is a very different thing than being attracted to someone. I glance at the corner and see Marcus is staring at me. That reinforces my desire to be close to this man, but the attraction is still surprising.

"What do you mean?"

"At the lake. You rescued six people."

His eyes grow wide and he says, "You were the one with the full glass."

"What?" I ask with a laugh.

"Everyone else was throwing drinks back like crazy. You were just sipping. I thought maybe you didn't want to be there."

I feel pretty damned awesome that he remembers me and again, it is strange to feel awesome. "You want to go somewhere a little quieter?"

He smiles and offers his arm. "My name is Fort."

I giggle. "Of course, it is."

He says, "Oh, making fun of my name. We're getting off to a great start."

I'm never like this but I giggle again and say, "What are you going to do, spank me?"

"Now that's an idea," he says with a smile as he puts a few bills on the bar top. I want to respond but I'm afraid I might humiliate myself by actually moaning at that.

"Thank you," I say. I intend to get control of myself but instead I pretty much giggle again. I'm like a completely flighty idiot at the moment.

In the parking lot, he says, "My car? Your car? Uber? Jogging shoes? You follow me? I follow you?" What the hell? I laugh like it's the funniest thing on Earth. For a moment, I think just being excited about something is so out of the ordinary for me that I'm almost giddy because of it. I don't know but I know I love feeling something again and the fact that it's a positive thing is wonderful.

"Well," I say, "that depends where we're going."

He smiles and then says, "Well, the quietest place I know is my condo."

I swear to God it makes no sense for me to suddenly

grow hornier than hell at the thought of going to his condo. For Christ's sake, I've known him for all of what? Five minutes? I just don't agree to such things so I have no idea why the hell I say, "I can get my car in the morning."

Jesus! In the morning... if there's any doubt about what will happen when we get to his place, it's gone now. For the love of God, what am I doing? On the other hand, if I knew getting out of this weird funk I've been in was a simple as going out and getting laid, I would have found someone to screw a long time ago. Damn, this man is the perfect man in that department.

We reach his place and make it about six inches past the door before we literally tear each other's clothes off. He is rough and aggressive but controlled and by the time we finally shed the last of our clothing, I need him so badly, I can't wait anymore.

"Please," I moan. "I need you inside me."

He snarls and lifts me up, carrying me to the bedroom. He throws me on the bed and I cry out with surprise and need. He approaches but instead of thrusting into me, he dives between my legs.

I gasp as all of my nerve endings seem to come alive. Pleasure shoots like sparks through my legs and up my spine and I gasp and writhe and stiffen as my body struggles to cope with the sensation. He explores me expertly, his lips and tongue working like magic through my folds and over my clit.

When the orgasm hits me, I scream and stiffen, then shudder as pleasure explodes through me like a series of grenades in my core, shooting through my whole body and rippling up and down my spine.

When I finally gain some semblance of control over my body, I cry out, "Oh, Fort, please, I need you inside me."

He snarls again, then slams into me so forcefully, my orgasm peaks again, even more powerfully than the first time. I shake underneath him uncontrollably, moaning and gasping as he continues to thrust.

The sheer size of the man is sexy as hell. His weight atop me is incredible and the way his cock stretches me out as he thrusts into me is the most physically satisfying thing I've ever felt. He moves sensually, with perfect control over his own body, like a predator pouncing on his prey.

I shudder as a third orgasm pulses through me and he cries out as his own climax takes him. I grind my hips over him as best I can with my own climax still roiling through me until I can't move anymore and jut lay underneath him, shaking and shivering.

I WAKE the next morning and know things are different. Today isn't like the other days. I'm not the girl I was the other days.

First, I just spent the night with a shifter. It all makes sense when I think over the night before. The way he snarls and grunts inside me, the animalistic way he moves, the almost superhuman prowess he showed rescuing the people on the houseboat the other day.

He stirs and I regard him while he sleeps. Even in sleep, a sense of power emanates from him. I softly lower my lips to his body and kiss him softly. I work my way down until I'm between his legs. He gasps when my mouth reaches its destination. I giggle and continue to suck until he groans and I feel his cock pulse in my mouth.

We have breakfast together and though we talk a lot, I don't bring up that he's a shifter. I don't work up the courage to ask him until that afternoon when he takes me back to my car and I turn to kiss him goodbye.

I wrap my arms around him but before our lips meet, I ask, "You're a shifter, aren't you?"

He grins but doesn't answer. Instead, he kisses me, deeply and passionately. My senses come alive again and I feel my nipples grow rock hard.

When he pulls away, I gasp. He walks back to his car, stops and turns to me. "I'm a wolf," he says.

Then he gets into his car and drives off.

I watch until he turns out of sight a few miles up the road. Then I get into my own car.

I catch sight of my face in the mirror as I step inside. I wear a huge grin that spreads from ear to ear.

I'm happy. The ennui is gone. I don't feel bored anymore.

I'm so happy, I forget all about seeing Marcus at the bar yesterday.

CHAPTER FOUR

Fort

I add a palmful of cumin to the pot and let the aroma wash over the kitchen like a tidal wave of comfort. Everything about my chili is bold. I don't mess around. There is something remarkable to me of never once making it in exactly the same way. Sure, I know the basic premises and I understand the techniques. That means I'm really just tweaking the recipe, never reinventing it. Still, there's enough variation it's something I love.

Does it make me an egotistical jerk that I no longer compete in chili contests because I got tired of winning every single one?

Well, I guess that's not the only thing that makes me an egotistical jerk anyway. The men are filtering in. They know chow time is just a few minutes away. Brett sees the two cast iron skillets of cornbread on the counter and says,

"Once again, I want to repeat my standing offer to let you do the cooking here all the time," as he grabs potholders and sets them on the dining room table.

"Not a chance," I say. With a chuckle, I add, "because then nobody would eat anyone else's food and wouldn't know how much better mine is."

"I don't know," he says, "I make a mean bowl of cereal."

"You'd burn the milk," Kurt says as he steps in. His face is covered with soot from drills. He walks through the kitchen to the sink in the mudroom and washes up.

"I'll be checking under your fingernails," I say.

"Shut up, wolfman," he says with a laugh.

Cliff steps in and says, "You fucking shifters. I swear to God, you think you're so damned cool." Everyone laughs at that one. His father is a shifter. His mother is not. With a shifter father and a non-shifter mother, there's a fifty-fifty chance. Shifter mothers always have shifter children. Of course, he's only twenty-eight. While most shifters gain their shifter nature around twelve, in very rare cases, it can happen as late as thirty-five.

"One of these days," I say, "you're going to turn into a bear and we'll all make you eat your words."

"If I turn into a bear, I'll kick all your asses," he replies and that leads to more laughter.

"Make yourself useful and help get the table set," I say.

Soon we're all at the table and the camaraderie is, like always, wonderful. I'm a little out of it, though. I can't get my one-night stand out of my head. Okay, that's kind of bullshit. I can't get the girl out of my head but I sure as hell hope it can be more than a one-night stand.

And I naturally make the mistake of asking, "So, how soon do you call a girl after?"

"After what?" Brett asks.

"After... well, we hung out last night and..."

Naturally, everyone goes crazy interrogating me. At least by the end I know I should reach out to her right away or tomorrow or three days from now or three hours ago or wait until she texts first or show up a few days from now unannounced or send her flowers or send her candy or show up at the bar where I first met her.

In other words, I have no fucking idea but now everyone is all up in my business.

Finally, Tommy asks the question I've been asking myself for the past ten minutes. "Dude, why would you ask that question here? You know we all have the collective maturity of a single twelve-year-old, right?"

"Speak for yourself," Brett retorts, "I'm a solid fifteen-and-a-half."

"Hey, hey, guys," Kurt interrupts. "I think we're all forgetting the most important question here." He leans close to me and says, "So what was it like? Is she good?"

I roll my eyes and stand. "All right, morons, you've made your point."

"Ooh, she must be *really* good!"

"Come on! At least tell me what she looks like!"

I stare thoughtfully at Kurt. "You know, she kinda looks like you."

The other firemen laugh and Kurt grins bashfully and says, "Well, gee, Fort, I think you're pretty too."

I chuckle. "Come on, who wants to watch the game before I leave you to languish without me?"

"No, no," Brett says. "You're not getting out of it that easily. Describe the lady, please."

"Uh, Brett, it's the playoffs," Tommy interjects. "I know girls are cool and all, but Beckett's on the mound tonight, so I think Fort's getting off with a warning and we can resume the interrogation tomorrow."

"Come on," Brett replies "Baseball or girls? Which is more interesting?"

"I mean, baseball season could end today," Tommy argues. "Girls will still be here tomorrow."

"Well, I'm watching the game," I say. I head to the tv room and spend the next three hours enduring a constant barrage of questions that I answer as cryptically as possible.

Beckett tosses a no-hitter and I manage to sneak out during the ensuing celebration and reach my car without enduring further teasing. I'm about to head home when I look in my backseat and see a jacket that belongs to Carmella.

My heart seems to lift, and I smile. Now I have a reason to go see her. My smile fades when I realize I don't know how to find her. I pick the jacket up, hoping to find a clue and as luck would have it, there's a receipt in one of the pockets that has an address on it.

I punch the address into my GPS and soon I am on my way. I feel a little weird finding her address on a receipt like that, but I comfort myself knowing I need to return her jacket one way or another and this is faster than mailing it.

The GPS leads to a working-class neighborhood a few miles from the lake. I reach the address and park across the street. The address belongs to a two-story apartment building of a common type with a few dozen units surrounding a long central courtyard.

The gate has a call box on it. I scroll through until I see, Bennett, Carm. and dial. There's no answer, so I try again. No answer once more. I feel my excitement start to fade, replaced with disappointment. Maybe I won't get to see her after all. I decide to try again and dial. A moment later, Carmella's voice answers suspiciously, "Hello?"

"Carmella," I say, "It's Fort. I have your jacket."

"Oh, Fort," she says. "How did you find my address?" Her voice is excited but there's a powerful sense of relief as well and I wonder why that might be.

"It was on a receipt in the jacket pocket. I hope I didn't offend you."

"Not at all," she says. "I'll buzz you in. Do you know my apartment number?"

"Fifteen, right?"

"Yes!" she says. "It's on the second floor."

She buzzes me in and I climb the stairs to the second

floor and look for fifteen. It's near the other side of the building and after a short walk. I stand in front of her door and ring the bell.

As soon as she opens the door, she throws her arms around me and kisses me. I let the jacket fall to the floor and wrap my arms around her.

She kisses me long and hard and when she pulls away, she looks at me with smoky eyes and says, "I missed you."

"I missed you too," I reply.

Then our arms are around each other once more.

CHAPTER FIVE

Carmella

This is sort of out of character for me. Actually, the first time was wildly out of character for me. This time is still out of character but it's almost like I'm just going all in. In the back of my mind, I'm a little bit worried. First and foremost, I'm worried that some of my emotions and my attraction comes from the knowledge that Fort can handle Marcus Holt. Marcus is a shifter, too, though he never told me and I never figured it out myself.

Unless him shifting and threatening me when I broke up with him counts.

Then I learned he was some kind of big cat. I wasn't thinking clearly but maybe a leopard or maybe a jaguar. Not sure.

Two years of never really feeling safe from Marcus Holt may have a lot to do with the whole ennui thing.

Perhaps I just can't engage this life the way I ought to, not when I have so much to worry about. Who knows? The bar a few days ago... First time seeing Marcus in two months. So, I'm afraid maybe I'm not being fair to Fort, that I'm pursuing a bodyguard and not a man.

"Jesus! Fort!" All of those thoughts disappear as his hands somehow magically drives me to distraction, one holding me to him between my shoulder blades and the other sliding down between my legs to rub at me through my clothing. Having no expectation of visitors, I wear thin drawstring lounge pants and a tee shirt with nothing else except my panties. My breasts feel especially sensitive and my nipples poke against the cotton and, pressed up against his broad chest, they seem particularly receptive to sensation.

I feel almost paralyzed and after two weeks of seeing this man on a regular basis, I suppose there isn't a damned thing I can do about my need for him. He deserves to know, though, and I force myself to push away from him. He looks at me, clearly confused. I say, "I need to get this out."

"All right," he's not sure how to take this and I can't blame him.

"When I first saw you, I was really turned on. That's all true. At the lake, I mean."

"Okay..."

"At the bar, I was glad to see you but part of why I went home with you was because I was afraid of my ex. I knew you were big and strong and could protect me from him."

He nods as though that isn't a big deal, which surprises me a little. Most men, even badass, strong, protective men, wouldn't be happy knowing a girl went home with them partially for protection from a violent ex. Fort, however, seems not only to take this in stride but to treat it as though it's a perfectly reasonable expectation. "Was he at the bar?" I nod and he asks, "Has he threatened you?"

I shake my head. "No. But... it's hard to explain."

"Just him being there threatened you."

I nod and he says, "Okay."

I quicjkly add, "And the night with you was incredible and every night with you has been incredible. I mean, not just the sex and..." I kind of slump and say, "And somewhere along the way it wasn't just because you're big and strong. It wasn't about your protecting me it was about... It is. I mean *is* about. I mean, I kind of went home with you because you could protect me but I'm with you now for other reasons."

"Okay," he says and steps back to me. He leans forward and kisses me and I back away.

"Didn't you hear me? I'm not being clear."

"Oh, sorry," he says. "How is this for a response? Holy shit, Carmella! How could you? You were scared and latched onto me because I could probably kick your ex-boyfriend's ass but then found out there was more to me and want me for other reasons? How terrible! Could you please get back to just thinking I'm badass?"

I giggle and he kisses me again. This time I don't back away.

He kisses me softly at first. Well, not exactly softly but he's definitely less aggressive than he was the night before. I wonder at first if he's afraid of being too rough with me, like maybe he'll trigger a bad memory of Marcus, so I pull away and whisper, "Fuck me," into his ear, hoping that by showing a little aggression of my own I can take away any reservations he might have.

Instead of instantly turning up the heat, he whispers back, "I will. I'm taking time to explore you."

To emphasize that point, he slides his hand back between my legs and begins massaging my pussy over my pants.

I moan and squirm over him as I feel my pussy get wet and my clit start to throb from his attention. His other hand holds me still so I can't try to move things faster and as my desperation grows, so does my pleasure. Incredibly, I am already close to orgasm but just before I cum, he moves his hand away from my pussy and allows it to travel over my navel, my thighs, my ass, and my breasts, moving with confidence but not aggression. I cry out and bite his shoulder softly as my climax peaks but doesn't quite release.

He holds my body still, so my hands begin to explore his body while he explores mine. God, he's built like a mountain! His chest is hard as granite and his abs feel like they're literally chiseled from marble. I lower my hand to the bulge in his pants and gasp. He's huge!

I know he's huge, of course. It's less than thirty-six hours since I've felt it and thirty-six years could pass and I still won't forget how incredible that experience was. Still, the restraint he shows and forces me to show intensifies every experience and my pussy pulses as I anticipate what it will feel like to have his huge cock push into me.

"Oh God, Fort, fuck me please!" I say.

He doesn't fuck me, but he does remove my shirt. A moment later, his mouth closes around my nipple and I cry out and shudder. God, I'm so ready! So ready, in fact, that when he slips his hand under my pants and slips a finger inside me, I cum immediately, so hard that I lose my feet. I don't fall because his other hand holds me up, allowing my climax to completely take over my body. I can't believe how good he feels and he hasn't even fucked me yet!

My orgasm seems to inspire him and finally, I hear him growl and his movements become more aggressive.

"Yes, Fort," I whisper as I undo his belt and unbutton his pants. "Take me. Make me yours."

That command breaks through the final ounce of restraint. He snarls and throws me onto the couch. I cry out, then cry out again as he yanks my pants and panties off.

Then I'm screaming and gasping and shuddering around his cock as he pounds me to greater physical heights than I've ever felt. I feel like I say that a lot: this is the hardest I've ever cum, the best I've ever felt, etc., etc. It's true though. Each time with him is better than everything I've ever experienced and only gets better.

Finally, he shudders and pulses inside me and I grind and squeeze and twist my pussy over him, desperate to make him cum. Not just cum. I want him to know that I'm his. My body belongs to him and its purpose is to make him feel good.

I've never wanted to belong to anyone before. I'm not sure how to feel about that, I just know that I want to be with him wherever the future takes me. I can't really tell him that after only two nights together, so instead, as we lay drifting toward sleep, I ask, "Where do you think this is going? Us, I mean."

"Everywhere," he says. "At least, I hope so."

"Me too," I say. Then I close my eyes and fall asleep to the rise and fall of his chest.

CHAPTER SIX

Fort

I walk the steps to Carmella's apartment grinning like a fool. The past four months with Carmella have easily been the best of my life. She's perfect and wonderful and though we're still in the honeymoon stage, I'm beginning to think she might be the one. Yeah, that's a lie. I know for a fact she's the one, and though I'm in no rush to walk down the aisle, I am sure that event is in our future.

Tonight, however, is just for fun. I'm going to order in and spend the evening alternating between holding her and screwing her to within an inch of your life. Sex isn't the only reason I love her, of course, but her almost insatiable drive is a nice cherry on top of what has turned out to be an incredibly delicious pie.

I knock on her door, grinning and hear her feet pounding as she rushes toward the door. To my utter shock, before she even opens the door, I hear her shout, "You asshole!"

I go from knocking on the door and excited to see her to completely stunned because she opens up and starts beating at my chest while she weeps. After four beautiful months with this girl, this is the first time I find myself completely unable to understand what's going on.

I don't know what the hell to do but I throw my arms around her and pull her tightly to me. I do it mainly to keep her from beating at my chest but it seems to work in other ways, too. Her body kind of melts into mine and she weeps without hitting anymore. I keep one arm wrapped around her and stroke her back softly.

The neighbor's door opens and I glance over there. It's a nice-looking old man and old lady. They smile at me and the man nods for me to bring Carmella into her apartment. I just mouth, "Thank you," and the old woman smiles. Carmella is still crying but softly now. I gently push her back into the apartment and lift her up, cradling her in my arms until I can set her down on the couch.

I gently disengage and get up. "I'm getting you a drink." I head to the kitchen and return with some water, a wine spritzer-like bottled drink, and a box of tissues from the counter. I set them down on the coffee table and then sit next to her. She puts her head in my lap and I stroke her shoulder as she cries for a bit and then finally says, "I... I saw you. I was... I was... I saw you and the Hoagland's next door saw you, too."

"Saw me? What did I do?"

"On television."

It takes about fifteen minutes for me to realize the fire at the extended education center on Twelfth Street got television coverage and that cameras rolled as I went back into the burning building over and over again to pull out high school kids who were trapped. I guess she watches television with the old couple next door every now and again. She is reeling and I guess part of the problem is the news program added to the drama, evidently declaring me dead three times when it took a while for me to return. They also got some expert or other to say going back and forth like that breaks the rules.

It does.

But I'm not the kind of guy who lets kids die for the sake of rules.

Anyway, she's still reeling because the news show shows me dying and then miraculously living three times and then when I go back in, they have to cut to the national news and she doesn't see me come back out. She spent the afternoon worrying about my death and feeling sad about it and angry at me for risking my life.

I want to reassure her and tell her that she doesn't need to worry about me ever, that I can handle situations like this, but she doesn't need me to tell her that right now. She needs me to hold her and stroke her hair and tell her everything's all right, so that's what I do. She sobs into my lap for a while. Eventually, she calms and I just hold her and stroke her hair for a while longer.

Finally, she sits up and mumbles, "I'm sorry. I was just—just so scared."

"I know, sweetheart."

"I thought you were dead."

"I know. I'm so sorry. Those news networks are the lowest form of life on Earth."

"Yeah, but—"

She doesn't finish, but I know what she's going to say.

"But why did I break the rules and keep going back in?"

She nods.

I take a moment before I answer. I want to present this in the most considerate way possible while also making it clear my position on the subject. I finally decide the best way to say it is just to say it.

"Carmella," I say, "I can't promise I'm not going to do that again."

She remains silent and I continue.

"I know I'm doing more than is expected of me. I know, I'm breaking rules but I can't let people die when I know I can save them."

"How do you know you can save them?"

"I know my limits. I know fires and I know firefighting. From the outside, it might look like I'm being reckless but I'm not. I know exactly what I can handle and I'll never put myself in a position I can't handle. But that means that sometimes I'm going to appear to be at more risk than I should be. I wish I could say it doesn't but I just can't watch people die for the sake of my own safety. I hope you can understand."

She doesn't respond at first. When she does, it's not with words. She leans toward me and kisses me, softly at first, then passionately. Soon, our clothes are off and not long after that, we're crying out and shuddering with our mutual climax.

She is calmer after that and we smile and talk and laugh like we usually do. Before we go to bed, she kisses me on the cheek, holds me tightly and says, "I understand. I won't lie and act like I'm thrilled by the fact that you're going to put yourself in harm's way a lot, but I understand. Just know that you have someone waiting for you when you come home."

That is probably the most beautiful thing I've ever heard.

We lie in bed a while and she chuckles.

"What's so funny?" I ask.

"Nothing," she says. "I just realized I haven't seen Marcus since that first day we met. I think maybe you scared him off."

"If he knows what's good for him," I say.

She giggles and snuggles up to me. Soon, I hear her soft regular breathing and know she's asleep.

I don't sleep right away.

I haven't told Carmella but after she first told me about Marcus, I tracked down Gael Donovan, an old acquaintance of mine who is a leopard shifter like Marcus. When I ask him about Marcus, he frowns. I tell him about the situation and he tells me that when he and the other leopards in the area heard about his threatening Carmella, they all warned him to back off.

There aren't really such things as alphas or leaders among shifters but just like with non-shifters, there are people who are respected at an elevated level in shifter society. Gael is one of those people for leopard shifters. A warning like that from him is to be taken seriously. So far, it seems like Marcus is taking it seriously.

I hope for his sake he continues to take it seriously.

CHAPTER SEVEN

Carmella

I feel guilty.

I suppose I should just be happy that I'm able to feel any emotion again and guilty is better than nothing. Still, I think Fort deserves more from me. He certainly deserves the truth from me, and the truth is our first time together had as much to do with me being concerned about seeing Marcus as anything else. Those aren't my feelings now, but I can't help but feel he deserves to hear this from me.

If there ends up being a confrontation, he'll come to his own conclusions.

I want to make sure he hears from me first.

Yeah, don't ask me why all of this comes to mind while I'm busy doing all I can to force myself to take all of his cock into my throat and holding tightly to his ass so my involuntary and instinctual need to pull back and breathe doesn't overcome my purpose.

I guess most men don't understand that most women let their minds wander during sex, even really good sex. Hell, I've had sex while trying to remember if I'm supposed to marinate the steak I'll be cooking tomorrow overnight or just a few hours. I've had sex going over all the potential problems I might deal with trying to negotiate the terms of my lease. I once tried to determine whether cupcakes or brownies made more sense for a birthday party at work, came hard, and in the midst of afterglow I decided on brownies.

But it's kind of strange while trying to make sure my lips reach the base of Fort's shaft and his balls rest right against my chin that I should be thinking about whether or not the origins of our relationship need to be addressed. I mean, I'm giving him deepthroat so it seems to me I'm mitigating any guilt that might belong on my shoulders.

But we had the whole conversation, didn't we?

I guess I kind of feel like it doesn't bother him as much as it should. Maybe he doesn't give me the kind of disapproval I need in order for these feelings to go away. Maybe it's just that I saw Marcus again earlier today when I was grocery shopping. He didn't say anything to me or approach me at all but he's still here and knowing that is enough to terrify me. Maybe it's just that he once again appears in my life and I...

That's it.

I resolve to talk to Fort about it.

I understand now.

My nose is pressed right up against Fort's pubic hair, his balls are on my chin and my throat is full.

And I understand.

My first thought about the sight of Marcus is gratitude for the relationship with Fort. That's what has me guilty. I'm naturally glad my boyfriend will beat the shit out the guy who threatens me. It's that simple. I'm naturally glad about that and it hearkens back to the kind of disingenuous beginning.

As he groans and I feel him swelling in my throat, it's like my mind returns right to the moment at hand and I press myself as far forward as I can as he cums.

"Jesus, Carmella," he exclaims.

He tries to push me away, but I push his hands away and begin sucking and bobbing eagerly, desperately. He moans and writhes, but I keep sucking and moaning and swallowing, suddenly desperate to make him cum again.

He snarls and forces my head away, then without slowing or stopping, lifts me off of the ground and drops me onto his cock.

My mouth flies open in a silent scream as he pounds me like a sledgehammer. I cum immediately but the climax doesn't represent the end of my pleasure but the beginning. My body stiffens, then shivers, then spasms as the orgasm strengthens until it reaches a nearly unbearable point.

Then it finally breaks and my scream becomes audible as I shudder over him. He keeps thrusting and grunting and the animal sounds he makes keeps my orgasm at its crest for several minutes after he empties himself inside me.

When the last powerful pulse of my orgasm finally subsides, I feel exhausted but overwhelmingly satisfied.

As we lay in each other's arms on the couch, I tell Fort that I saw Marcus today.

He frowns and adopts a protective expression that is as wonderfully sexy as it is reassuring. "You did?" he asks, his voice low and dangerous. "Where?"

"At the supermarket," I say.

He sits up and stares intently at me. "What happened? Did he say anything to you?"

I shake my head. "No. I just saw him there."

"Did he see you?"

I nod. "Yes, he saw me. I caught him looking at me from across the produce section."

His eyes narrow and I add, "He didn't say anything. He looked at me for a few minutes, then continued to shop."

"Did he see you get into your car? Did he see which way you went when you left the store?"

"No, I don't think so. I think he was just shopping and happened to run into me. It just freaked me out a little."

He takes my hands in his and leans forward until he is inches from my face. He speaks softly, but there is steel behind his gentleness. "Carmella, listen to me. You don't need to worry about Marcus anymore. If he tries anything: talking to you, approaching you, even looking at you funny, you tell me and I'll make sure he never bothers you again. If you see him again, you tell me and I'll make him understand that you are so far off limits he shouldn't even be in the same county as you. You understand?"

His earnestness and protectiveness is as titillating as it is reassuring. I run my hands along his thighs and say, "I understand. Thank you."

Then I lower myself to my knees. I'm not as aggressive as I am earlier, but the noises he makes tell me he doesn't enjoy it any less.

CHAPTER EIGHT

Fort

Shifters like Holt piss me off.

Sure, there are assholes in any group of individuals. That goes for shifters and non-shifters. There are also assholes within each particular race of shifters.

Holt is worse.

There is a level of morality that goes with being a shifter, that mitigates our animal nature enough to make us humane even if we'll never be fully human. Wolf shifters might beat the shit out of each other and wolves and bears might go toe to toe every now and then. There's an assumption of relative strength, though. A wolf shifter who goes after an ocelot shifter—yes, there are ocelot shifters—would be universally shunned the same way you might despise an owner of a dog who sics the animal on kittens. In the case of a shifter, though, the shifter himself (or herself) becomes the owner and the animal and... Well, you get the point.

However, there is an argument to be made that the strong preying on the weak within the shifter community is just the natural state of things. So, shunning a shifter who preys on a weaker shifter is a lot like how a group of college kids shun a douchebag. It isn't the end of the world and maybe in a few years, the guy turns over a new leaf.

Shifters using their animals to hurt or threaten humans isn't tolerated at all.

There are a number of reasons for this, and they're not just moral. They're practical, too. The reality is if all shifters transformed right this moment and went to war against humanity, it would be a very short war. We wouldn't win. We'd be extinct. Sheer numbers would ensure that but also technology. We don't tend to technological advancement. In fact, even decked out with the best combat gear, a Navy SEAL who is also a shifter finds it very hard to use anything other than fists in the midst of battle.

And various shifters over the years preyed on humans.

Werewolves. Vampires. Bugbears. Boogeymen. All of those monsters come from the actions of shifters and they're the reason we spent centuries in hiding. Attacking or threatening humans threatens all shifter kind.

Plus, the prick is threatening a woman I love. Well, maybe I love her.

No, I definitely love her.

The way I encapsulate all of this right now makes it seem like I'm thinking rationally. The reality is all the thoughts just swirl around my head as I head into the station and make a beeline to the back, where I'm hoping Jeff O'Leary is still helping a group of volunteer firefighters visiting from three states away for training.

He's there, and as though God smiles on me at the moment, I hear him say, "Okay, everyone. Great job. Sorry but you've got bullshit for the rest of the afternoon down in city hall. Hit the showers and then we'll see you all tomorrow morning."

I wait five or ten minutes as they say their goodbyes. Finally, Jeff sees me he gives me a nod in greeting and I step up as he finishes his goodbyes to the last of the men. "What's up, dog?"

"What's up with you, cat?"

Those phrases are the same as, "Hello," for the two of us.

"I got a leopard problem," I say.

"Yeah?"

"You know a guy name Marcus Holt?"

I can tell immediately by the look on Jeff's face that he does. I know every wolf shifter in a five-hundred-mile radius. The total population of wolves is about five times as large as the leopard shifters so it's not all that surprising.

"Is he in jail again?" Jeff asks.

"No," I say. "Is he often in jail?"

Jeff nods. "He's a well-known screw up among the leopard community. From what I understand, he threatened a girl a year or so ago and now no one will talk to him anymore."

"That's right," I confirm. "That girl is my girl."

Jeff's eyes widen. "He threatened *your* girl?"

I nod. "Carmella is Marcus's ex-boyfriend. She broke up with him when he became violent and he shifted into his leopard and threatened to kill her. She ran away but he found her and he's been lurking here ever since."

Jeff's jaw tenses and his hands ball into fists. "That fucking little prick. I should've torn his throat out when I had the chance."

He bares his teeth when he speaks and I see his canines start to lengthen and his pupils contract into slits. He closes his eyes and takes a deep breath and when he opens his eyes, his pupils are round again. "So," he says. "Marcus is back in town and he's threatening his ex, who is your girl now."

I nod. "To be fair, he hasn't exactly threatened her yet. She's seen him around but he hasn't approached her or said anything to her yet."

"Yeah, but it's leading to that," Jeff says and any sliver of hope I had that Carmella and I might be overreacting disappears as Jeff continues. "That's his MO. He wants his prey to see him stalking them. He gets off on fear. I've seen it. Even when he's hunting, he'll do something to give himself away so he can chase the deer or boar or whatever down and hear them squeal. He's a sadistic little monster and Carmella is very lucky that she found you."

"So there won't be any trouble if I have to handle the situation?"

Jeff nods grimly. I don't explicitly say it, but it's clear what I mean by *handle the situation.* I don't advocate violence, even the tolerated level of mild shifter-on-shifter violence, but when someone threatens someone I care about, as far as I'm concerned, all bets are off. It doesn't surprise me that Jeff feels the same way.

"There won't be any trouble," he says. "But I'll run it by Gael just to be sure. You know Gael?"

I nod. "I know him. I actually spoke to him a few months ago about Marcus. He told me he warned Marcus to back off of Carmella, so I let it drop until she saw him again yesterday."

"Well, he'll want to know that his favorite fuckup is fucking up again."

He dials a number and puts the phone on speaker, then sets it on the table. A moment later, Gael answers, "Jeff, Jeff, banana-nana-fo-feff, me-my-mo—"

"Sorry to interrupt your outstanding display of comedy," Jeff interjects, "But I'm here with a wolf friend of mine, Fort Gilmore."

Immediately, Gael understands. "Marcus being a dipshit again?"

"Yep," Jeff confirms. "Looks like he's still harassing his ex."

I hear a low growl on the other end of the line. "I told that prick to back off already."

"Looks like he didn't take it seriously enough."

"Well, you tell your wolf friend he should feel free to do whatever he needs to do to keep this asshole away from his girlfriend. He won't have to worry about retaliation from me or any of the other leopards."

"You're on speaker; you can tell him yourself."

"Oh, good. Fort, you there?"

"I'm here, Gael."

"Yeah, we're done with Marcus. He's been a problem his whole life and he clearly has no plans to stop. You do what you need to do and don't worry about anyone making life difficult for you. I'll spread the word that Marcus is no longer considered a part of our community. Jeff, can you let the leopards in your area know?"

"Most of them know already, but I'll tell them just the same."

"Thank you. Fort, I'm not kidding. You do whatever you have to do to stop this guy. Whatever that means."

"I appreciate it, Gael," I say. "You can consider this problem taken care of."

"Glad to hear it." He pauses a moment. "This is kind of a dumb thing to ask but if you get a chance and it's not too weird, can you mention to Carmella that not all of us are like this? Leopards, I mean. I know it's cheesy but we've worked hard to be accepted, like all shifters, and it sucks to know that a guy like Marcus Holt could put a stain on that reputation."

"She knows," I say. "But she'll appreciate knowing you said something."

"Thank you, really appreciate it."

After Gael hangs up, Jeff turns to me. "I'm pretty sure you can handle a stain like Marcus Holt without any help but if you do happen to want assistance, call me, yeah?" He grins and his pupils start to narrow again as he growls. "At the very least, I'll get to see him put in his place."

I smile grimly. "I'll keep you posted."

I leave feeling reassured. I wasn't worried about catching heat from the leopards but it's nice to know everyone has my back if it does come down to this.

For Marcus' sake, I hope it doesn't.

CHAPTER NINE

Carmella

As I put the lipstick on, I giggle at my reflection. I don't usually dress up. Well, I'm not exactly dressed up. I don't think I have the courage to leave the house this way. I'm wearing a very thin cotton summer dress in a very light shade of pink. I have thigh high stockings and short heels. That's it for clothing. If I stand by a window, the outline of my body will be very evident.

I wear only enough eye liner to make my eyes pop and I wear deep crimson lipstick.

Ultimately, I'm dressed up unless *up* means dressed to fuck.

No, it isn't a slutty look but I don't imagine anyone could possibly mistake my purpose.

"Girl, you're going to drive that boy wild," Kim says from behind me. I smile and mess up the lip color.

"Hush!" Diane says. She turns me to face her, wipes off my lipstick, and then starts applying it to my lips herself. "Nevermind. Talk all you want but let me handle the lips." It's interesting to see the studiousness of my friend's expression as she applies the lipstick. I know the minimalist approach to the makeup will make my lips seem extraordinarily alluring.

I can almost see the bulge in Fort's pants growing.

It takes a lot of effort to stay still and finally she pulls back, grabs a tissue and blots. She smiles and says, "Are you sure you don't want a little blush?"

Kim says, "I don't think so. Right now she's got that contradiction going?"

"Contradiction?" I ask.

Kim turns me so I look at my reflection. "You don't look made up. It doesn't look like you put any makeup on and yet your eyes and those damned lips. The point is, you're innocent and fuckable all at once."

"No shit," Diane says, "This is going to be a pretty damned good anniversary for Fort."

"It's only a six-month anniversary," I say.

"Oh yeah," Kim says, "not important at all. That's why you called us over to help you get doled up and why you've got a crown roast of lamb about to go into the oven. That's right. No big deal at all."

Diane says, "Yeah, should I go find a pair of granny panties and a comfy bra for you to slip on?"

I giggle and lift my hands in surrender. "Okay, okay. You made your point."

"Well," Kim says, "Get that roast in the oven."

I walk from the bathroom and she lands a slap on my ass like I'm a football player and she is my coach. I yelp, and she points a finger at me with a fake glare. "I get the next shifter. Period. Me."

There's laughter about that, of course. We walk out to the kitchen and soon, the lamb is in the oven and the table is set. The lamb will cook and hour and rest for twenty minutes. Kim pours wine and the two toast me and my anniversary. They help me with final touches and just when I get the roast out and cover it with foil to rest, the hug me goodbye and leave.

It is sometimes hard for me to remember that just six months ago, I walked through life like it was nothing, like I existed but there was nothing past the existence that made any sense at all to me or, for that matter, gave me any reason for happiness. I can't recall really feeling anticipation back then. Now, though, the knowledge my man... my wolf man... will be here any minute now has me desperately excited.

When the knock comes at the door, I giggle. "Big fireman forgot his key," I say as I walk there. "Dummy!" I say as I pull open the door.

All of my energy disappears.

Every ounce.

This is why I don't flee as desperately as I want to flee. Marcus stands in front of me, his mouth twisted up in a sinister smile and his eyes dark and evil. "You think you can humiliate me?" he asks. He steps forward and I finally find my legs and leap back. His arms darts out, though and he catches my wrist, twisted it so I almost fall over. "You didn't have the right to leave me in the first place," he says, "and it's time you come back where you belong."

"Let go of me," I whimper. "Stop."

He laughs and says, "I've decided I want cubs, and that means you'll be producing a number of litters."

I pull back and he yanks my arm. The pain as he twists my wrist is extraordinary. He laughs again and yanks me toward him so I fall against his chest. He smells musty and rancid and my skin crawls with revulsion as well as fear.

"Come on, Carmella," he says, "Don't pretend you don't like it. You remember how I used to make you scream?"

The memory of that—that *monster* on top of me is enough to make me physically ill. I wretch and try to pull away again but he yanks me back and uses his other hand to force my head up so he can whisper in my ear as he forces himself inside the apartment and closes the door, "Does your *human* make you scream too? Does he make you shiver like me?"

"Please," I whisper.

His response is to twist my head so I face him and try to force a kiss on me.

Then he throws himself backward, crashing into the wall with a cry of pain and collapsing to the floor.

I am confused for a moment.

Then I see Fort.

He stands protectively in front of me, lips bared in a snarl. "You will not touch her again," he growls.

And I know I will be safe. I am still frightened, so much so that I shrink against the wall and hug my knees to my chest, but through my fear, I know that I'll be okay. Fort is here and he'll protect me.

Marcus growls and comes up swinging. Fort easily sidesteps the blow and sends his fist crashing into the side of Marcus's head. Marcus drops again and lies still and I feel a rush of hope that this is finally over.

Then I hear the sound of fabric ripping and watch in horror as Marcus shifts.

He gets to his feet and stares at Fort, hate and evil in his yellow cat's eyes. He growls, crouches, and then leaps.

CHAPTER TEN

Fort

Of all shifters, wolves are the ones least able to control themselves when it comes time to shift. A lot of people think there's something romantic about us. Let me tell you something. Forget everything you've ever read or heard about wolves. Did you know the whole alpha wolf concept was debunked years ago? In fact, it's all bullshit and it's all the fault of chickens.

Yeah, you heard me. Chickens.

In the twenties, studies were done with chickens and agriculturalists detected a social structure. Essentially, if you're a chicken, you can peck chickens in a lower position on the social hierarchy. You can't peck chickens on a higher position. This is how the term *pecking order* came about. Well, that concept went all throughout the natural sciences and naturalists observing wolves noticed a social structure.

And IMMEDIATELY dismissed it as something that only happened in captivity. In the wild, what seemed like a wolf pack was usually two parents and their pups. This idea of fighting for dominance to become the alpha is just absolute bullshit. Of course, some rebellious and unfortunately uneducated wolf shifters took up the idea and to this day there are shifter packs that run like the completely debunked and idiotic concept of an alpha wolf.

Frankly, I think they just like that it turned on human housewives and provided them with some eager and happy breeders.

Anyway, that's an idiotic shifter politics thing more than anything else. My point is that wolf shifters in general have less control than other shifters. Why is that? It's simple. Wolves are killers. Plain and simple, wolves are killers. That's what we are. We're the apex predator everywhere we are. Everything about us is designed to hunt and kill. Further, we're not social animals. We're not even pack animals. In the wild wolves have monogamous couples that pretty much mate for life and if you see five or six together, any other than the two are their kids.

We're designed to kill.

Sorry if that isn't as romantic as some hierarchy that puts a sexy alpha at odds with a beautiful young woman who refuses to be more than just a womb. It's the truth, though.

Wolf shifters are, by nature, killers, too. However, our human nature mitigates a great deal of that. However, if a bear shifter gets angry, he's not likely to shift into a bear unwillingly. If a tiger shifter gets pissed, she's not going to transform without actively desiring it. About the closest you'll get to a shifter who has no real choice but to shift when angry is a dragon shifter. There are instinctual shifts, of course. There are some eagle shifters and if you push one off a cliff, he'll shift even if he intends to commit suicide. It takes a great effort for a horse shifter not to shift if she happens to be running at full speed.

For wolves, most of our teaching as teenagers involves training to keep from getting pissed off. This is because wolves get pissed off and shift naturally whether or not we want to.

Unfortunately for this unmitigated asshole, I want to.

By the time he launches himself at me in his leopard form, my snout is already extending and my teeth are lengthening and sharpening into canines. I dodge his leap and he turns to me, confused. His eyes widen as he watches my clothes tear and my legs and arms transform to huge paws while fur sprouts all over my body. I realize he didn't know I'm a shifter.

I use the surprise to my advantage and launch at him, snapping at his throat. He recovers in time to move his throat away from my jaws, so I catch his rear right paw by the ankle instead. I bite down and shake my head, tearing at the tendons and ligaments.

Marcus shrieks in pain and the sound of his scream

and the feel of my prey's flesh ripping and tearing in my jaws drives the last shred of humanity from me. I am no longer human. I am a wolf. I am a predator and the leopard in front of me has threatened my mate.

There is only one end for an animal that threatens my mate.

He snarls and swipes at me with a huge paw. I release his rear ankle and snap at the paw he swipes at me with. I feel my fangs pierce his flesh again, hear his cry of pain and mixed with it, fear. The fear is like fuel to my rage and I press my attack, snapping and tearing and slicing at him.

On paper, a leopard should have a significant advantage against a wolf in a one-on-one fight. Both animals are about the same size, although shifters are much larger in their animal forms than the actual animals they shift into and Marcus and I are no exception. Leopards, however, are solitary animals and built for one-on-one confrontation as a result, able to use all four paws as weapons in addition to their teeth and generally being more agile than a wolf. Wolves, in contrast, usually hunt in groups and are designed to wear their prey down over long distances and a long period of time before finally moving in for the kill.

The on-paper advantage doesn't matter here, however. Marcus Holt threatened my mate. It doesn't matter if he's a wolf, a leopard, or a brown bear. He threatened my mate and he will die for that.

He swipes at me with powerful paws but I easily avoid them, darting in and out and snapping at his paws and shoulders and his soft belly. None of the wounds I inflict are fatal but they take their toll and over the next few minutes, the one paper advantage I do have becomes clear. Leopards, like most solitary predators, are designed to kill quickly. Their bodies are optimized for a brief burst of energy followed by a long rest period. Wolves will sometimes chase prey for days without tiring.

His movements become slower and more predictable and I know the end is near. I see the fear in the leopard's eyes and know he realizes the end is near as well.

In a final, desperate act, he lunges for my neck. I side-step but not quite far enough and his fangs sink into my shoulder. I snarl from the pain but the pain doesn't slow me. I shake my forelegs powerfully and throw him off of me. He falls on his back in the kitchen. He scrabbles for purchase but the tile floor makes it difficult for him to gain traction and he doesn't regain his feet in time to avoid my next and final attack.

My jaws clamp around his throat and I bite down hard, savoring the taste of blood and the brittle crack of the bones in his throat. He flails his paws, struggling to escape but it's too late. With a growl, I twist my head and tear his throat out.

The leopard makes a horrible, wet choking sound and continues to flail, his movements slowing as life ebbs from his body. After a few moments, he shifts and the leopard is replaced with the surprised, fearful face of Marcus Holt.

His eyes glaze over and I lick my lips, anticipating the

meal to come. I take two steps toward my prey, then hear a noise from the living room.

I turn and see Carmella, eyes wide with fear, huddling in the corner near the door.

And my humanity returns.

I blink and groan as my limbs reorganize themselves. The fur covering my body retreats and my snout flattens. My teeth diminish and flatten to fit my human jaw and a moment later, I stand in the kitchen, covered in blood and tattered clothing, the last remaining indication of the animal I was only a moment ago.

Carmella looks at me, wide-eyed, and I say, "It's over. You're safe now."

CHAPTER ELEVEN

Carmella

I don't even have a frame of reference for how things feel. On one level, I think I'm in shock because of the violent nature of what I just saw. There's a great deal of horror right now. I feel sick and weak inside, kind of like if I almost fall or something and get filled with adrenaline that then disappears and leaves me weak and almost nauseas afterward. That's the kind of sick feeling I have right now over the shock of the violence witnessed.

At the same time, I'm so utterly flooded with relief. A big portion of that relief is the knowledge I need never fear Marcus again. Maybe I'm a bad person to be happy he's dead. Maybe I'll end up feeling guilty for being happy about it later. I don't know. For right now, though, I feel like I have a brand-new lease on life, a lease unencumbered by the absolutely terrible fear that has filled me for far, far too long. The largest part of the relief though is that Fort is unhurt.

Most of all, and this makes me a very strange person, I'm aroused.

Yeah, I'm horny as hell.

Can you imagine a therapist trying to get to the bottom of that?

I suppose it's natural that my gratitude for what Fort did along with my relief that he's okay explains at least part of my arousal. Of course, the fact that he's the most sexually attractive human being on Earth has to be considered, too. He's amazing and he's here and he just changed my life even more than before.

And I want to fuck him.

Let's put this in perspective.

He stands, breathing heavily, his face and chest covered with blood. One of his shoulders is covered with blood as well. Marcus is on the floor, his throat torn open in a grotesque display of violence. I just witnessed a giant wolf kill a giant... I suppose a leopard. I just saw it and the images of that battle are the most savage images in the entirety of my experience.

And I want to fuck Fort.

Something's wrong with me, no doubt about it.

Fort turns his head and looks at me. "It's over," he says. "You're safe now."

I don't say anything for a moment and he asks, "Are you okay?"

I nod, still unable to speak. Finally, I manage, "Are you?"

"I'm fine," he says.

The dam breaks and the tears fall as I rush over to him, throwing my arms around him and holding tightly to him as I weep against his chest. I realize my carefully chosen summer dress is getting covered with blood and I just don't care. I don't ever want to let go. I hold Fort as tightly as I can and his arms around me offer me such dramatic comfort I feel like my world is finally coming back together.

God, despite all of this strangeness, I feel normal again.

I weep for a long time. I really don't know why I'm weeping. I weep well past the point at which the tears of relief are through. I weep and while I do, I wonder what the hell I'm weeping about. I think maybe if there really are three parts to a person, a body and soul and spirit, I'm weeping in order to cleanse all of them. My body is fine now and if my soul is the brain, that's fine as well. As for my spirit, maybe that weeps.

Oh, who the hell knows? I'm not a philosopher. I'm a girl who's safe because of the man she loves. "I love you," I whisper.

He pushes me back just enough to lift my face with a finger under my chin. "I love you, too," he says and I realize this is the first time the two of us declare our love for each other.

I giggle. He looks confused and it makes me giggle

more. I finally manage to say, through laughs, "Our first... our first... the first time we tell each other we love each other. You're covered with blood and I'm not wearing panties!"

He looks confused for another second and then he starts laughing, too. Finally, though, he pushes me back and says, "I need you to go clean up. Take a long shower and leave your dress on the floor outside of the bathroom. Do it now."

Something in his tone makes anything other than disobedience impossible. I nod and walk toward the bedrooms. I have to pass the sliding glass door and I wonder idiotically if the silhouette of my body is visible with the sundress.

I take the dress off and hope Fort is watching me get naked. I giggle at the absurdity of the thought and enter the shower.

The warm water calms my raging emotions and as I slowly wash away the sweat and blood and fear, the sense of normalcy becomes stronger and with it the assurance that the fear that has followed me for the past year is finally gone.

I am safe.

I leave the shower and see the sundress is gone. Fort must have taken it while I showered.

I dress in shorts and a t-shirt and return to the living room. Now that the fear of death is passed, my thoughts turn to cleaning the mess in my living room. It's not possible that the neighbors didn't hear the fight and when the police show up and see Marcus dead and Fort covered in blood, it might be difficult to convince them the killing was justified.

I enter the living room and stop. My eyes widen in shock.

The living room is spotless. Marcus is gone, as is every trace of blood on the floor, the walls, the furniture, everywhere. The apartment is spotless, as though the fight never happened. The only sign that it ever occurred is the blood that still covers Fort, who stands naked in front of me, his own clothes, or what remains of them, taken to be disposed of along with my dress.

"What—How—" I begin.

"The shifter community takes care of its own," Fort explains. "I told the other leopards that I would need to deal with Marcus and they gave me their blessing. While you were in the shower, I called them and they cleaned up."

I nod. After everything I've seen, the idea that there were other leopard shifters waiting to help Fort protect me from Marcus isn't surprising at all.

I undress in front of Fort and am pleased to see his eyes narrow with lust. There will be time to indulge that later, however. Right now, we need to get him cleaned up.

I lead him to the shower and wash him, taking extra care around the wound in his shoulder. He relaxes slowly. When he is clean, I lower myself to my knees and take my time rewarding him for saving my life. His climax is my climax as well, the climax to a story that began with an ill-advised liaison with a murderous leopard and ends with a beautiful relationship with my beautiful, strong wolf.

EPILOGUE

Carmella

I think it might take me some time to really wrap my head around feeling things on a regular basis. It's strange to wake up excited. I guess to an extent, this reminds me of what I was like five or ten years ago but the truth is, I don't believe I ever really felt like life was something beautiful and engaging. I suppose I never really believed life was something wonderful, to be enjoyed. At least, I never felt that actively, anyway.

Everything feels differently now.

I take a moment to appreciate then when I open my eyes and see just the first glowing light of dawn filtering through the gauzy curtains on the window. I take a breath and as I let it out, I'm smiling. I glance to my left and see the digital display of my nightstand clock. It's just before six. In a few weeks, Daylight savings time will spring forward and dawn will come later.

I cannot recall feeling excited and happy in the morning for a very long time.

I see the reason when I turn my head to the right and see my man sleeping there. Perhaps that's the wrong way to say that. I turn my head to the right and see my wolf sleeping there. That works a little better. How in the world am I supposed to describe him, to think about him? Perhaps I can't. Perhaps I will just have to think of it as turning my head to the right and seeing Fort sleeping there.

No.

My Fort.

Mine.

He's mine, and that makes life wonderful.

I really ought to let him sleep.

But I also really ought to enjoy him before things are too unwieldy. I very carefully lift the blanket and slide off the bed. I creep around to the foot of the bed and then climb up. Fort tends to kick the blankets off at night, and that's perfect for me right now. He lies with his legs spread slightly, just enough for me to climb on and make it up to mid-thigh without touching him. I carefully slide my arms under his thighs and he murmurs softly in his sleep.

A moment later, he murmurs not so softly as my lips close over his cock and I feel him growing in my mouth. I recall conversations with my friends. Kim always talks about giving head as a power trip. Diane always talks about it like a beautiful gift that's romantic and sensual. I guess I fall somewhere in between. I love the intimacy of the act and I love the feeling of control it gives me.

Sometimes, the sweetness and intimacy war with the sense of control for supremacy and there are times I feel a tremendous thrill about how powerful it makes me to have a man completely at my mercy because of sensations I deliver. At other times, those same sensations make me feel loving and generous and beautiful.

Then, there are times like now, when doing this makes me feel a sense of love and joy along with a sense of security that's very powerful and beautiful. At the same time, though, I feel a tremendous amount of power. It's like every movement of my tongue is some kind of magic trick. No! It's like I'm a puppet master and my tongue and lips are how I move the strings.

There is no man in my experience that can come even close to the power and strength of Fort. Nonetheless, a slight movement of my lips, a tiny increase in the suction, or a flick of my tongue beneath the head of his cock as I move my head can elicit any response I want. If I want a sigh, I can move slowly and feel the energy seeping from his body. If I want a gasp, I can plunge deeply. If I want a plaintive moan that begs me without words for more, I can draw figure eights along the underside of his shaft with the tip of my tongue.

I can even drive him to the point where he can't just passively receive. I can between intense sensations for him and then light sensations that aren't intense at all. I can truly drive him to a point of desperation focusing only on the tip until he can't help but grab the back of my head and push me deeper. I love having control and feeling the control. I love all that but I particularly love that I can simply give him pleasure and extend it as long as possible before he cums.

He cums and wakes as he does. I push him deep in my throat and suck deeply and sensually from the base of his shaft to the tip, watching his eyes as I do.

"Jesus, Carmella!" he cries.

I don't stop until his cock finished pulsing in my throat. I tilt my head back so he can see me swallow, then smile at him. "Good morning, Mr. Gilmore."

He chuckles. "Good morning, Mrs. Gilmore."

My stomach lurches and I grimace and put a hand on my swollen belly.

He sits up, concerned, and I smile and say, "I'm all right. The cubs are just a little restless today."

He returns my smile and lays a hand on my belly to feel them kick. The wonder and joy on his face are price-less. I could stare at him all day.

He notices my stare and looks at me, smiling. He lifts his hand from my belly and softly caresses my face. "I love you, Carmella," he says.

"I love you too," I say.

We embrace and as my husband's strong arms wrap around me I realize for the hundredth time in the past year that my life is perfect.

I am his and he is mine.

What more could a girl want?

DID you like *Reckless Wolves Dangerous Liaison?* I've written a great many shifter romances and Fort might be my absolute favorite leading man, or should I call him a leading wolf? I fell in love with him while I wrote this and I hope you did as well. Did you think there would have to be a final confrontation with Marcus Holt? I kind of feel like he got what was coming to him. What do you think? I also have to say that I agree with Kim. The next shifter is mine!

Here's some good news! The company 417 shifters aren't going anywhere. In the next book, you're in for a real treat. What do you get when a government inspector decides it's her job to audit the operations of Company 417 and a no-nonsense polar bear shifter is her point of contact? Sparks! That's what you get. Tabitha Greene isn't the kind of government inspector to mess around. She's caught corruption in office after office and enters into a job expecting it. As for Rory Eise, he doesn't give a damn how beautiful this woman is. He's not going to stand for a constant accusatory tone. Of course, when the chips are down, and they always are for these sexy fireman shifters, there's nothing either of them can do to resist what comes naturally. Will it work out for them? Find out in *Wild Bear's White-Hot Romance,* the next sexy and exciting tale in the always romantic and steamy *Company 417 Shifters* Series!